Priestess of th

Sewell Peaslee Wright

Alpha Editions

This edition published in 2024

ISBN 9789362094339

Design and Setting By

Alpha Editions
www.alphaedis.com

Email - info@alphaedis.com

As per information held with us this book is in Public Domain.
This book is a reproduction of an important historical work.
Alpha Editions uses the best technology to reproduce historical work
in the same manner it was first published to preserve its original nature.
Any marks or number seen are left intentionally to preserve.

Priestess of The Flame

I have been rather amused by the protests which have come to me regarding the "disparaging" comments I have made, in previous tales of the Special Patrol Service, regarding women. The rather surprising thing about it is that the larger proportion of these have come from men. Young men, of course.

Now, as a matter of fact, a careful search has failed to reveal to me any very uncomplimentary remarks. I have suggested, I believe, that women have, in my experience, shown a sad lack of ability to understand mechanical contrivances. Perhaps I have pictured some few of them as frivolous and shallow. If I have been unfair, I wish now to make humble apology.

I am not, as some of my correspondents have indicated, a bitter old man, who cannot remember his youth. I remember it very well indeed, else these tales would not be forthcoming. And women have their great and proper place, even in a man's universe.

Some day, perhaps, the mood will seize me to write of my own love affair. That surprises you? You smile to think that old John Hanson, lately a commander of the Special Patrol Service, now retired, should have had a love affair? Well, 'twas many years ago, before these eyes lost their fire, and before these brown, skinny hands wearied as quickly as they weary now....

But I have known many women—good women and bad; great women and women of small souls; kindly women, and women fierce as wild bears are fierce. Divinity has dealt lavishly with women; has given them an emotional range far greater than man's. They can sink to depths unknown to masculinity; they can rise to heights of love and sacrifice before which man can only stand with reverently bowed head and marvel.

This is a story of a woman—one of those no man could know and not remember. I make no apologies for her; I pay her no homage. I record only a not inaccurate account of an adventure of my youth, in which she played a part; I leave to you the task of judging her.

We were some three days out from Base, as I recall it, on a mission which promised a welcome interlude in a monotonous sequence of routine patrols. I was commander then of the *Ertak*, one of the crack ships of the Service, and assisted by the finest group of officers, I believe, that any man ever had under him.

I was standing a watch in the navigating room with Hendricks, my junior officer, when Correy brought us the amazing news.

Correy was my first officer, a square-jawed fighting man if one ever breathed, a man of action, such as these effete times do not produce. His eyes were fairly blazing as he came into the room, and his generous mouth was narrowed into a grim line.

"What's up, Mr. Correy?" I asked apprehensively. "Trouble aboard?"

"Plenty of it, sir!" he snapped. "A stowaway!"

"A stowaway?" I repeated wonderingly. A new experience, but hardly cause for Correy's obvious anger. "Well, send him below, and tell Miro to put him to work—the hardest work he can find. We'll make him—"

"*Him?*" blurted Correy. "If it were a him it wouldn't be so bad, sir. But it's a *she*!"

To understand the full effect of the statement, you'd have to be steeped in the traditions of the Service. Women are seldom permitted on board a ship of the Service; despite their many admirable qualities, women play the very devil with discipline. And here were we, three days out from Base on a tour of duty which promised more than a little excitement, with a female stowaway on board!

I felt my own mouth set grimly.

"Where is she, Mr. Correy?" I asked quietly.

"In my quarters, under guard. It was my watch below, as you know, sir. I entered my stateroom, figuring on catching forty winks, and there she was, seated in my big chair, smiling at me.

"Well, for a second I couldn't speak. I just stared at her, and she kept smiling back at me. 'What are you doing here?' I managed to ask her, at last. 'Do you know where you are?'

"'I'll talk to your commanding officer,' she told me, cool as you please. 'Will you bring him, please?'

"'You'll see him plenty soon enough,' I snapped at her, getting over my surprise somewhat by that time. I called in a couple of men to keep her from getting into mischief, and reported to you. What are your orders, sir?"

I hesitated a second, wondering. From Correy's account, she must be a rather remarkable person.

"Bring her up here, if you will, Mr. Correy. I'd like to see her before we put her in the brig." The brig, I might explain, was a small room well forward, where members of the crew were confined for discipline.

"Right, sir!" It seemed to me that there was a peculiar twinkle in Correy's eyes as he went out, and I wondered about it while we waited for him to return with the prisoner.

"What an infernal nuisance, sir!" complained Hendricks, looking up from his glowing charts. "We'll be the laughing-stock of the Service if this leaks out!"

"*When* it leaks out," I corrected him glumly. I'd already thought of the unpleasant outcome he mentioned. "I'll have to report it, of course, and the whole Service will know about it. We'll just have to grin and make the most of it, I guess." There was still another possibility which I didn't mention: the silver-sleeves at Base would very likely call me on the carpet for permitting such a thing to happen. A commander was supposed to be responsible for everything that happened; no excuses available in the Service as it was in those days.

I scowled forbiddingly as I heard Correy open the door; at least I could make her very sorry she had selected the *Ertak* for her adventure. I am afraid, however, that it was a startled, rather than a scowling face to which she lifted her eyes.

"This is the stowaway, sir," said Correy briskly, closing the door. He was watching my face, and I saw, now, the reason for the twinkle in his eye when I mentioned placing the stowaway in the brig.

The woman was startlingly beautiful; one of the most beautiful women I have ever seen, and I have roamed the outer limits of space, and seen the women of many worlds. Hendricks, standing behind me, gasped audibly as his eyes fell upon her.

The stowaway was regally tall and exquisitely modeled. Her hair was the color of pale morning sunlight on Earth; her eyes an amazing blue, the equal of which I have never seen.

She was beautiful, but not coldly so. Despite her imperious bearing, there was something seductive about the soft curves of her beautiful body; something to rouse the pulses of a man in the langour of her intensely blue eyes, and the full, sensuous lips, scarlet as a smear of fresh blood.

"So this is the stowaway," I said, trying to keep my voice coolly indifferent. "What is your name?"

"I should prefer," she replied, speaking the universal language with a sibilant accent that was very fascinating, "to speak with you privately."

"You will speak with me," I informed her crisply, "in the presence of these officers. I repeat: what is your name?"

She smiled faintly, her eyes compelling mine.

"I am called Liane," she said. "Chief Priestess of the Flame. Mother of Life. Giver of Death. I believe my name and position are not unknown to you, Commander Hanson?"

Known to me? If Base was not in error—and for all their faults, the silver-sleeves are seldom wrong in matters of this sort—this woman was the reason for our present mission.

"They are known to me," I admitted. "They do not explain, however, your presence here."

"And yet they should," protested Liane gently. "I was taken from my own people by those who had no right to command me. I was subjected to the indignity of questioning by many men. I have merely taken the simplest and quickest way of returning to my own people."

"You know, then, our destination?"

"I was informed of that by those who questioned me," nodded Liane. "Then, since I had been assured I was an honored guest, and no prisoner, I secreted myself aboard the ship, hiding in a small room nearly filled with what I took to be spare parts. I had provisions, and a few personal belongings. When I felt sufficient time had elapsed to make a return improbable, I donned attire more fitting than the masculine workman's guise in which I had secreted myself, and—I believe you are acquainted with the remaining facts."

"I am. I will consider your case and advise you later. Mr. Correy, will you conduct the stowaway to my quarters and place her under guard? Return when you have attended to this matter, and ask Mr. Kincaide to do likewise."

"To your quarters, you said, sir?" asked Correy, his eyes very serious, but not sufficiently so to entirely disguise the twinkle in their depths. "Not to the brig?"

I could cheerfully have kicked him.

"To my quarters," I repeated severely, "and under guard."

"Right, sir," said Correy.

While we were awaiting Correy and Kincaide, I briefly considered the rather remarkable story which had been told me at Base.

"Commander Hanson," the Chief of Command had said, "we're turning over to you a very delicate mission. You've proved yourself adept at handling matters of this kind, and we have every confidence you'll bring this one to a highly successful conclusion."

"Thank you, sir; we'll do our best," I had told him.

"I know that; the assurance isn't necessary, although I appreciate it. Briefly, here's what we're confronted with:

"Lakos, as you know, is the principal source of temite for the universe. And without temite, modern space travel would be impossible; we would have to resort to earlier and infinitely more crude devices. You realize that, of course.

"Now, for some time, those in charge of operations on Lakos have complained of a growing unrest, increasing insubordination on the part of the Lakonians, and an alarming decrease in production.

"It has been extremely difficult—indeed, impossible—to determine the reasons for this, for, as you are perhaps aware, the atmosphere of Lakos is permeated with certain mineral fumes which, while not directly harmful to those of other worlds, do serve to effectively block the passage of those rays of the sun which are essential to the health of beings like ourselves. Those in charge of operations there are supplied artificially with these rays, as you are in your ship, by means of emanations from ethon tubes, but they have to be transferred at frequent periods to other fields of activity. The constant shifting about produces a state of disorder which makes the necessary investigation impossible. Too, operations are carried on with an insufficient personnel, because it is extremely difficult to induce desirable types of volunteer for such disagreeable service.

"We have, however, determined a few very important facts. This unrest has been caused by the activities of a secret organization or order known as the Worshipers of the Flame. That's as close a translation as I can give you. It sounds harmless enough, but from what we gather, it is a sinister and rather terrible organization, with a fanatical belief amounting, at times, to a veritable frenzy. These Lakonians are a physically powerful but mentally inadequate people, as perhaps you are aware.

"The leader of this order or cult call it what you will—seems to be a woman: a very fascinating creature, infinitely superior to her people as a whole; what biologists call a 'sport,' I believe—a radical departure from the general racial trend.

"This leader calls herself Liane, Chief Priestess of the Flame, Mother of Life, Giver of Death, and a few other high-sounding things. We have called her here to Base for questioning, and while she has been here some time, we have so far learned next to nothing from her. She is very intelligent, very alluring, very feminine—but reveals nothing she does not wish to reveal.

"Our purpose in having her brought here was two-fold: first, to gain what information we could from her, and if possible, prevail upon her to cease her activities; second, to deprive her cult of her leadership while you conducted your investigation.

"Your orders, then, are simple: you will proceed at once to Lakos, and inquire into the activities of this order. Somehow, it must be crushed; the means I shall leave to you. You will have complete coöperation of those in charge of operations on Lakos; they are Zenians and natives of Earth, and you may depend upon them implicitly. Do not, however, place any faith in any Lakonians; the entire native populace may well be suspected of participation in the rites of this cult, and they are a treacherous and ruthless people at best. Have you any questions, Commander?"

"None," I had told him. "I have full authority to take any action I see fit?"

"Yes, at your discretion. Of course," he had added rather hastily, "you appreciate the importance of our supply of temite. Only Lakonians can gather it in commercial quantities, under the existing conditions on Lakos, and our reserve supply is not large. We naturally wish to increase production there, rather than endanger it. It's a delicate mission, but I'm trusting you and your men to handle it for us. I know you will."

He had arisen then, smilingly, and offered his hand to me in that gesture which marks a son of Earth throughout the universe, thus bringing the interview to a close.

In talking the things over with my officers, we had decided the mission promised to be an interesting one, but full of difficulties. The *Ertak* had set down on Lakos more than once, and we all had unpleasant memories of the place.

The sunlight on Lakos, such as it was, was pale green and thin, lacking in warmth and vitality. The vegetation was flaccid and nearly colorless, more like a mushroom growth than anything else; and the inhabitants were suspicious and unfriendly.

Remembering the typical Lakonians, it was all the more surprising that a gracious creature like Liane could have sprung from their midst. They were a beetle-browed, dark race, with gnarled muscles and huge, knotted joints, speaking a guttural language all their own. Few spoke the universal language.

But Liane, Chief Priestess of the Flame! The image of her kept drifting back to my mind. There was a woman to turn any man's head! And such a turning would be dangerous, for Liane had no soft woman's soul, if I had read her brilliant blue eyes aright.

"Rather a beauty, isn't she, sir?" commented Hendricks as I paused in my restless pacing, and glanced at the two-dimensional charts.

"The stowaway? Rather," I agreed shortly. "And chief instigator of the trouble we've been sent to eliminate."

"That seems almost—almost unbelievable, doesn't it?"

"Why, Mr. Hendricks?"

Correy and Kincaide entered before my junior officer could reply. I think he was rather glad of the excuse for not presenting his reasons.

"Well, sir, she's under guard," reported Correy. "And now what's to be done about her?"

"That," I admitted, "is a question. After all, she's an important personage at home. She was brought to Base as a guest, probably something of a guest of honor, of the Council, I gather. And, considering the work that's cut out for us, it would seem like a poor move to antagonize her unduly. What do you gentlemen think?"

"I think you're right, sir," said Hendricks quickly. "I believe she should be given every consideration."

Kincaide, my level-headed second officer, glanced curiously at Hendricks. "I see she's made one friend, anyway," he said. "Don't let yourself slip, my boy; I've run across her kind before. They're dangerous."

"Thanks, but the warning's not necessary, Mr. Kincaide," replied Hendricks stiffly, an angry flush mounting to his checks. "I merely expressed a requested opinion."

"We'll let that phase of it drop, gentlemen," I cut in sharply, as I saw Kincaide's eyes flash. Trust a woman to stir up strife and ill-feeling! "What shall we do with her?"

"I believe, sir," said Correy, "that we'd be nice to her. Treat her as an honored guest; make the best of a bad situation. If she's what the Chief thought she is, the boss of this outfit we've got to lick, then there's no need of stroking her the wrong way, as I see it."

"And you, Mr. Kincaid?"

"I see no other way out of it. Under the circumstances, we can't treat her like a common culprit; both her position and her sex would prevent."

"Very well, then; we seem to be agreed. We'll find suitable quarters for her—"

"I'll give her mine," put in Hendricks. "Correy will let me double up with him, I imagine."

"Sure," nodded Correy.

Kincaide glanced sharply at Hendricks, but said nothing. I knew, however, that he was thinking just what I was: that my young third officer was in for a bad, bad time of it.

Just how bad, I think neither of us guessed.

Liane became a member of the officers' mess on the *Ertak*. She occupied Hendricks' stateroom, and, I must confess, with uncommon good judgment for a woman, remained there most of the time.

She knew the reason for our mission, but this was one subject we never discussed. Nor did we mention the sect of which, according to the Chief of Command, she was the head. We did talk freely, when brought together at the table, on every other general topic.

Liane was an exceedingly intelligent conversationalist. Her voice was fascinating, and her remarks were always to the point. And she was a very good listener; she paid flattering attention to the most casual remark.

It seemed to me she was particularly gracious to Hendricks. Her strangely arresting blue eyes seldom left his face when he was speaking, and the greater portion of her remarks seemed addressed to him. Naturally, Hendricks responded as a flower responds to the warming rays of the sun.

"We'll do well, sir, to keep a weather eye on the youngster," opined Correy one morning. (I think I have previously explained that even in the unchanging darkness of space, we divided time arbitrarily into days and nights). "Unless I'm badly mistaken, Hendricks is falling victim to a pair of blue eyes."

"He's young," I shrugged. "We'll be there in two more days, and then we'll be rid of her."

"Yes," nodded Correy, "we'll be there in a couple of days. And we'll be rid of her, I hope. But—suppose it should be serious, sir?"

"What do you mean?" I asked sharply. I had been thinking, rather vaguely, along much the same lines, but to hear it put into words came as rather a shock.

"I hope I'm wrong," said Correy very gravely. "But this Liane is an unusual woman. When I was his age, I could have slipped rather badly myself. Her eyes—that slow smile—they do things to a man.

"At the same time, Liane is supposed to be the head of the thing we're to stamp out; you might say the enemy's leader. And it wouldn't be a good thing, sir, to have a—a friend of the enemy on board the *Ertak*, would it?"

A rebuke rose to my lips, but I checked it. After all, Correy had no more than put into words some fears which had been harassing me.

A traitor—in the Service? Perhaps you won't be able to understand just what that thought meant to those of us who wore the Blue and Silver in those days. But a traitor was something we had never had. It was almost unbelievable that such a thing would ever happen; that it could ever happen. And yet older men than Hendricks had thrown honor aside at the insistence of women less fascinating than Liane.

I had felt the lure of her personality; there was not one of us on board the *Ertak* who had not. And she had not exercised her wiles on any of us save Hendricks; with the shrewdness which had made her the leader she was, she had elected to fascinate the youngest, the weakest, the most impressionable.

"I'll have a talk with him, Mr. Correy," I said quietly. "Probably it isn't necessary; I trust him implicitly, as I am sure you do, and the rest of us."

"Certainly, sir," Correy replied hastily, evidently relieved by the manner in which I had taken his remarks. "Only, he's very young, sir, and Liane is a very fascinating creature."

I kept my promise to Correy the next time Hendricks was on watch.

- 9 -

"We'll be setting down in a couple of days," I commented casually. "It'll be good to stretch our legs again, won't it?"

"It certainly will, sir."

"And I imagine that's the last we'll see of our fair stowaway," I said, watching him closely.

Hendricks' face flushed and then drained white. With the tip of his forefinger he traced meaningless geometrical patterns on the surface of the instrument table.

"I imagine so, sir," he replied in a choked voice. And then, suddenly, in a voice which shook with released emotion. "Oh, I know what you're thinking!" he added. "What you've all been thinking; you, sir, and Correy and Kincaide. Probably the men, too, for that matter.

"But it's not so! I want you to believe that, sir. I may be impressionable, and certainly she is beautiful and—and terribly fascinating; but I'm not quite a fool. I realize she's on the other side; that I can't, that I must not, permit myself to care. You—you do believe that, sir?"

"Of course, lad!" I put my hand reassuringly on his shoulder; his whole body was shaking. "Forget it; forget her as soon as you can. None of us have doubted you for an instant; we just—wondered."

"I could see that; I could feel it. And it hurt," said my junior officer with shame-faced hesitancy. "But I'll forget her—after she's gone."

I let it go at that. After all, it was a rather painful subject for us both. The next day it did seem that he treated her with less attention; and she noticed it, for I saw the faint shadow of a frown form between her perfect brows, and her glance traveled meditatively from Hendricks' flushed face to my own.

The next morning, after the first meal of the day, she walked down the passage with me, one slim white hand placed gently within the curve of my arm.

"Mr. Hendricks," she commented softly, "seems rather distraught the last day or so."

"Yes?" I said, smiling to myself, and wondering what was coming next.

"Yes, Commander Hanson." There was just the faintest suggestion of steeliness in her voice now. "I fancy you've been giving him good advice, and painting me in lurid colors. Do you really think so badly of me?" Her hand pressed my arm with warm friendliness; her great blue eyes were watching me with beseeching interest.

"I think, Liane," I replied, "that Mr. Hendricks is a very young man."

"And that I am a dangerous woman?" She laughed softly.

"That, at least," I told her, "your interests and ours are not identical."

"True," she said coolly, pausing before the door of her stateroom. Her hand dropped from my arm, and she drew herself up regally. In the bright flow of the ethon tubes overhead she was almost irresistibly beautiful. "Our interests are not identical, Commander Hanson. They are widely divergent, directly opposed to each other, as a matter of fact. And—may I be so bold as to offer you a bit of advice?"

I bowed, saying nothing.

"Then, don't attempt to meddle with things which are more powerful, than you and the forces you control. And—don't waste breath on Mr. Hendricks. Fair warning!"

Before I could ask for more complete explanation, she had slipped inside her stateroom and firmly closed the door.

We set down on Lakos late that afternoon, close to the city—town, rather—of Gio, where those in charge of operations made their headquarters. With Liane and Correy, leaving the ship in charge of Kincaide, I made my way quickly toward the headquarters building.

We had gone but a few steps when Liane was surrounded by a shouting throng of her fellow Lakonians, and with a little mocking wave of a white hand, she stepped into a sort of litter which had been rushed to the scene, and was carried away.

"For one," commented Correy with a sigh of relief, "I'm glad she's out of sight. If I never see her again, it'll be too soon. When do we start something?"

"Not until we've talked with Fetter, who's in command here. I have a letter for him from the Chief. We'll see what he has to say."

One thing was certain; we could look for no assistance of any kind from the natives. They regarded us with bleak scowls, from beneath shaggy, lowering brows, our uniforms of blue, with the silver ornaments of our service and rank, identifying us clearly.

In the greenish Lakonian twilight, they were sinister figures indeed, clothed all alike in short, sleeveless tunics, belted loosely at the waist, feet and legs encased in leather buskins reaching nearly to the knees, their brown, gnarled limbs and stoop-shouldered postures giving them a half-bestial resemblance which was disturbing. Their walk was a sort of slow shuffle, which made their long arms dangle, swinging disjointedly.

We entered the administration building of gray, dull stone, and were ushered immediately into the office of the head of operations.

"Hanson?" he greeted me. "Mighty glad to see you. You too, Correy. Terrible hole, this; hope you're not here for long. Sorry I couldn't meet you at the ship; got your radio, but couldn't make it. Everything's in a jam. Getting worse all the time. And we're shorthanded; not half enough men here. Sit down, sit down. Seem good to feel firm ground under your feet?"

"Not particularly; your air here isn't as good as the *Ertak's*." Correy and I seated ourselves across the desk from the garrulous Fetter. "I've a letter here from the Chief; I believe it explains why we're here."

"I can guess, I can guess. And none too soon. Things are in terrible shape. Terrible." Fetter ripped open the letter and glanced through it with harried eyes.

"Right," he nodded. "I'm to help you all I can. Place myself at your disposal. What can I do?"

"Tell us what's up," I suggested.

"That would be a long story. I suppose you know something about the situation already. Several reports have gone in to Base. What did the Chief tell you, Hanson?"

Briefly, I sketched the Chief's report, Fetter nodding every few words. When I had finished, he rubbed his long, thin fingers together nervously, and stared down, frowning at the littered top of his desk.

"Right as far as he went," he said. "But he didn't go far enough. Wanted you to find out for yourself, I suppose.

"Well, there *is* a secret society working against us here. Sect, I'd call it. Undermined the whole inhabited portion of Lakos—which isn't a great area, as you know."

"The Chief Priestess is Liane. I believe you said she stowed away on the *Ertak* with you?"

I nodded.

- 12 -

"You're keeping her under guard?" asked Fetter.

"No; under the circumstances, we couldn't. We had no authority, you see. A crowd of natives bore her away in triumph."

"Then your work's cut out for you," groaned Fetter. "She's a devil incarnate. Beautiful, irresistible, and evil as corruption itself. If she's back, I'm afraid there's nothing to be done. We've been sitting on a volcano ever since she left. Pressure growing greater every instant, it seemed. She's just what's needed to set it off."

"We'll have to take our chances," I commented. "And now; just what is the set-up?"

"The Worshipers of the Flame, they call themselves. The membership takes in about every male being on Lakos. They meet in the great caverns which honeycomb the continent. Ghastly places; I've seen some of the smaller ones. Continent was thrust up from the sea in a molten state, some scientific chap told me once; these caverns were made by great belches of escaping steam or gas. You'll see them.

"She—Liane—and her priests rule solely by terror. The Lakonians are naturally just horses" (a draft animal of ancient Earth, now extinct), "content to work without thinking. Liane and her crew have made them think—just enough to be dangerous. Just what she tells them to think, and no more. Disobedient ones are punished by death. Rather a terrible death, I gather.

"Well, her chief aim is to stop the production of temite. She wishes to bargain with the Council—at her own terms."

"What's her price?" I asked. "What does she want, wealth?"

"No. *Power!*" Fetter leaned forward across the desk, hammering it with both fists to emphasize the word, his eyes gleaming from their deep sockets. "Power, Hanson, that's what she craves. She's insane on the subject. Utterly mad. She lusts after it. You asked her price; it's this: a seat in the Council!"

I gasped audibly. A seat in the Council! The Council, composed of the wisest heads of the universe, and ruling the universe with absolute authority!

"She *is* mad," I said.

"Crazy," grunted Correy. "Plain crazy. A woman—in the Council!"

Fetter nodded solemnly.

"Mad—crazy—use your own terms," he said. "But that's her price. The Chief didn't tell you that, did he? Well, perhaps he didn't know. I learned it in a very roundabout way. She'll make the formal demand when the time is ripe, never fear. And what's more, unless these Worshipers of the Flame are stamped out—*she'll get what she demands!*"

"Impossible!"

"Not at all. You know what this place is. Only a Lakonian can stand this atmosphere long. No vitality to the light that does come through this damned green stuff they breathe for air; and after a few days, the acid, metallic tang of it drives you frantic. Never can get used to it.

"So the Lakonians have to mine the temite. And the universe must have temite, in quantities that can't be supplied from any other source. If the Lakonians won't mine it—and they won't, when Liane tells them to quit— what will the Council and your Service do about it?"

"Plenty," growled Correy.

"Nothing," contradicted Fetter. "You can kill a man, disintegrate him, imprison him, punish him, as you will, but you can't make him work." And there that phase of the matter rested.

I asked him a number of questions which I felt would help us to start our work properly, and he answered every one of them promptly and fully. Evidently, Fetter had given his problem a great deal of thought, and had done more than a little intelligent investigating of his own.

"If there's anything else I can do to help you," he said as he accompanied us to the door, "don't fail to call upon me. And remember what I said: trust no one except yourselves. Study each move before you make it. These Lakonians are dull-witted, but they'll do whatever Liane tells them. And she thinks fast and cunningly!"

We thanked him for his warning, and hurried back to the ship through the sickly-green Lakonian dusk. The acrid odor of the atmosphere was already beginning to be disagreeable.

"Decent sort of a chap, Fetter," commented Correy. "All wrought up, isn't he? Worried stiff."

"I imagine he has cause to be. And—he might have been right in saying we should have held Liane: perhaps we could have treated with her in some way."

"No chance! Not that lady. When we treat with her, we'll have to have the whip hand, utterly and completely."

The heavy outer door of the *Ertak's* exit was open, but the transparent inner door, provided for just such an emergency, was in place, forming, in conjunction with a second door, an efficient air-lock. The guard saw us coming and, as we came up, had the inner door smartly opened, standing at salute as we entered. We returned his salute and went up to the navigating room, where I proposed to hold a brief council of war, informing Kincaide and Hendricks of what we had learned from Fetter, and deciding upon a course of action for the following day. Kincaide, whom I had left on watch, was there waiting.

"Well, sir, how do things stack up?" he asked anxiously.

"Not so good. Please ask Mr. Hendricks to report here at once, and I'll give you the whole story."

Kincaide pressed the attention signal to Hendricks' room, and waited impatiently for a response. There was none.

"Try my room," suggested Correy. "Maybe he hasn't moved back to his own quarters yet."

"That's what he said he would be doing," replied Kincaide. But that signal too failed to bring any response.

Correy glanced at me, a queer, hurt expression in his eyes.

"Shall I go forward and see if he—if he's ill?" he asked quickly.

"Please do," I said, and as soon as he was gone I turned to the microphone and called the sentry on duty at the exit.

"Commander Hanson speaking. Has Mr. Hendricks left the ship?"'

"Yes, sir. Some time ago. The lady came back, saying she had word from you; she and Mr. Hendricks left a few minutes later. That was all right, sir?"

"Yes," I said, barely able to force the word from between my lips. Hendricks ... and Liane? Hendricks ... a traitor? I cut the microphone and glanced at Kincaide. He must have read the facts in my eyes.

"He's ... gone, sir?"

"With Liane," I nodded.

The door burst open, and Correy came racing into the room.

"He's not there, sir!" he snapped. "But in his room I found this!"

He held out an envelope, addressed to me. I ripped it open, glanced through the hasty, nervous scrawl, and then read it aloud:

"Sir:

I am leaving with Liane. I am sorry. It had to be.

Hendricks."

"That, gentlemen," I said hoarsely, after a long silence, "will make the blackest entry ever spread upon the log of the *Ertak*—upon any ship of the Service. Let us dismiss this thing from our minds, and proceed."

But that was easier, by far, to propose than to accomplish.

It was late indeed when we finished our deliberations, but the plan decided upon was exceedingly simple.

We would simply enforce our authority until we located definite resistance; we would then concentrate our efforts upon isolating the source of this resistance and overcoming it. That we would find Liane at the bottom of our difficulties, we knew perfectly well, but we desired to place her in a definite position as an enemy. So far, we had nothing against her, no proof of her activities, save the rather guarded report of the Chief, and the evidence given us by Fetter.

There were three major continents on Lakos, but only one of them was inhabited or habitable, the other two being within the large northern polar cap. The activities of The Worshipers of the Flame were centered about the chief city of Gio, Fetter had told us, and therefore we were in position to start action without delay.

Force of men would avail us nothing, since the entire crew of the *Ertak* would be but a pitiful force compared to the horde Liane could muster. Our mission could be accomplished—if, indeed, it could be accomplished at all—by the force of whatever authority our position commanded, and the outwitting of Liane.

Accordingly, it was decided that, in the emergency, all three of us would undertake the task, leaving the ship in charge of Sub-officer Scholey, chief of the operating room crew, and a very capable, level-headed man. I gave him his final instructions as we left the ship, early the next morning:

"Scholey, we are leaving you in a position of unusual responsibility. An emergency makes it necessary, or at least desirable, for Mr. Correy, Mr. Kincaide and myself to leave the ship. Mr. Hendricks has already departed; therefore, the *Ertak* will be left in your charge.

- 16 -

"Remain here for five days; if we do not return in that time, leave for Base, and report the circumstances there. The log will reveal full authority for your actions."

"Very well, sir!" He saluted, and we passed through the air-lock which protected the *Ertak* from the unpleasant atmosphere of Lakos, armed only with atomic pistols, and carrying condensed rations and menores at our belts.

We went directly to the largest of the mines, the natives regarding us with furtive, unfriendly eyes. A great crowd of men were lounging around the mouth of the mine, and as we approached, they tightened their ranks, as though to block our passage.

"We'll bluff it through," I whispered. "They know the uniform of the Service, and they have no leader."

"I'd like to take a swing at one of them," growled Correy. "I don't like their looks—not a bit. But just as you say, sir."

Our bluff worked. We marched up to the packed mass as though we had not even noticed them, and slowly and unwillingly, they opened a path for us, closing in behind us with rather uncomfortable celerity. For a moment I regretted we had not taken a landing crew from the *Ertak*.

However, we won through the mouth of the mine without violence, but here a huge Lakonian who seemed to be in authority held up his hand and blocked our way.

"Let me handle him, sir," said Correy from the corner of his mouth. "I understand a little of their language."

"Right," I nodded. "Make it strong!"

Correy stepped forward, his head thrust out truculently, thumbs hooked through his belt, his right hand suggestively near his automatic pistol. He rapped out something in unpleasant gutturals, and the tall Lakonian replied volubly.

"He says it's orders," commented Correy over his shoulder. "Now I'll tell him who's giving orders around here!"

He stepped closer to the Lakonian, and spoke with emphatic briefness. The Lakonian fell back a step, hesitated, and started to reply. Correy stopped him with a single word, and motioned us to follow him. The guard watched us doubtfully, and angrily, but he let us pass.

"He told me," explained Correy, "that *she* had given orders. Didn't name her, but we can guess, all right. I told him that if she wished to say anything to us, she could do it in person; that we weren't afraid of her, of him, or all the Lakonians who ever breathed green soup and called it air. He's a simple soul, and easily impressed. So we got by."

"Nice work," I commended him. "It's an auspicious start, anyway."

The mouth of the mine was not the usual vertical shaft; as Fetters had told us, it was a great ramp, of less than forty-five degrees, leading underground, illuminated by jets of greenish flame from metal brackets set into the wall at regular intervals, and fed by a never-failing interplay of natural gas. The passageway was of varying height and width, but nowhere less than three times my height from floor to ceiling, and it was broad enough at its narrowest so that ten men might have marched easily abreast.

The floor, apparently, had been smoothed by human effort, but for the rest, the corridor was, to judge from the evidence, entirely natural for the walls of shiny black rock bore no marks of tools.

At intervals, other passages branched off from the main one we were following, at greater and less angles, but these were much narrower, and had very apparently been hewn in the solid rock. Like the central passage, they were utterly deserted.

"We'll be coming out on the other side, pretty soon," commented Correy after a steady descent of perhaps twenty minutes. "This tunnel must go all the way through. I—what's that?"

We paused and listened. From behind us came a soft, whispering sound, the nature of which we could not determine.

"Sounds like the shuffle of many feet, far behind," suggested Kincaide gravely.

"Or, more likely, the air rushing around the corners of those smaller passages," I suggested. "This is a drafty hole. Or it may be just the combined flarings of all these jets of flame."

"Maybe you're right, sir," nodded Correy. "Anyway, we won't worry about it until we have to. I guess we just keep on going?"

"That seems to be about all there is to do; we should enter one of the big subterranean chambers Fetters mentioned, before long."

As a matter of fact, it was but a minute or two later, that we turned a curve in the corridor and found ourselves looking into a vast open space, the roof supported by huge pillars of black stone, and the floor littered with rocky debris and mining tools thrown down by workmen.

"This is where they take out the temite ore, I imagine," said Kincaide, picking up a loose fragment of rock. He pointed to a smudge of soft, crumbly gray metal, greasy in appearance, showing on the surface of the specimen he had picked up. "That's the stuff, sir, that's causing us all this trouble: nearly pure metallic temite." He dropped the fragment, looking about curiously. "But where," he added, "are the miners?"

"I'm inclined to believe we'll find out before we get back to the *Ertak*," said Correy grimly. "Everything's moved along too sweetly; trouble's just piling up somewhere."

"That remains to be seen," I commented. "Let's move on, and see what's beyond. That looks like a door of some sort, on the far side. Perhaps it will lead us to something more interesting."

"I hope it does," growled Correy. "This underground business is getting on my nerves!"

It was a door I had seen, a huge slab of light yellow-green metal. I paused, my hand on the simple latch.

"Stand to one side," I said softly. "Let's see what happens."

I lifted the latch, and the heavy door opened inward. Cautiously, I stared through the portal. Inside was blackness and silence; somewhere, in the far distance, I could see two or three tiny pin-pricks of green light.

"We'll take a look around, anyway," I said. "Follow me carefully and be ready for action. It seems all right, but somehow, I don't like the looks of things."

In single file, we passed beyond the massive door, the light from the large room outside streaming ahead of us, our shadows long and grotesque, moving on the rocky floor ahead of us.

Then, suddenly, I became aware that the path of light ahead of us was narrowing. I turned swiftly; the door must be closing!

As I turned, lights roared up all around us, intense light which struck at our eyes with almost tangible force. A great shout rose, echoing, to a vaulted ceiling. Before we could move or cry out, a score of men on either side had pinioned us.

- 19 -

"Damnation!" roared Correy. "If I only had the use of my fists—just for a second!"

We were in a great cavern, the largest I have ever beheld. A huge bubble, blown in the molten rock by powerful gases from the seething interior of the world.

The roof was invisible above our heads, and the floor sloped down gently in every direction, toward a central dais, so far away that its details were lost to us. From the center of the dais a mighty pillar of green flame mounted into the air nearly twenty times the height of a man. All around the dais, seated on the sloping floor of the cavern, were Lakonians.

There were hundreds of them, thousands of them, and they were as silent and motionless as death. They paid no heed to us; they crouched, each in his place, and stared at the column of greenish flame.

"It was a trap," muttered Kincaide as our captors marched us rapidly toward the dais in the center of the huge amphitheater. "They were waiting for us; I imagine we have been watched all the time. And we walked into the trap exactly like a bunch of schoolboys."

"True—but we've found, I believe, what we wished to find," I told him. "This is the meeting place of the Worshipers of the Flame. There, I imagine is the Flame itself. And unless I'm badly mistaken, that's Liane waiting up there in the center!"

It was Liane. She was seated on a massive, simple throne of the greenish-yellow metal, the column of fire rising directly behind her like an impossible plume. In a semicircle at her feet, in massive chairs made of the odd metal, were perhaps twenty old men, their heads crowned with great, unkempt manes of white hair.

And standing beside Liane's throne, at her right hand, was—*Hendricks!*

His shoulders drooped, his chin rested upon his breast. He was wearing, not the blue-and-silver uniform of the Service, but a simple tunic of pale green, with buskins of dark green leather, laced with black. He did not look up as we were ushered before this impressive group, but Liane watched us with smiling interest.

Liane, seated there upon her throne, was not the Liane of those days in the *Ertak*. There, she had been scarcely more than a peculiarly fascinating young woman with a regal bearing and commanding eyes. Here, she was a goddess, terrifyingly beautiful, smiling with her lips, yet holding the power of death in the white hands which hung gracefully from the massive arms of the throne.

She wore a simple garment of thin, shimmering stuff, diaphanous as finest silk. It was black, caught at one shoulder with a flashing green stone. The other shoulder was bared, and the black garment was a perfect foil for the whiteness of her perfect skin, her amazing blue eyes, and the pale gold of her hair.

She lifted one hand in a slight gesture as our conductors paused before the dais; they fell away and formed a close cordon behind us.

"We have awaited your coming," she said in her sibilant voice. "And you are here."

"We are here," I said sternly, "representing, through our Service, the Supreme Council of the universe. What word shall we take back to those who sent us?"

Liane smiled, a slow, cruel smile. The pink fingers of one hand tapped gently on the carven arm of her throne. The eyes of the semicircle of old men watched us with unwavering hatred.

"The word you carry will be a good word," she said slowly. "Liane has decided to be gracious—and yet it is well that you have full understanding of Liane's power. For while the word Liane shall give you to bear back is a good word, still, Liane is but a woman, and women have been known to change their minds. Is that not so, Commander Hanson?"

"That is so, Liane," I nodded. "And we are glad to hear that your wisdom has led you to be gracious."

She leaned forward suddenly, her eyes flashing with anger.

"Mark you, it is not wisdom but a whim of mine which causes me to be graciously minded!" she cried. "Think you that Liane is afraid? Look about you!"

We turned slowly and cast our eyes about that great gathering. As far as the eye could reach, in every direction, was a sea of faces. And as we looked, the door through which we had entered this great hall was flung open, and a crowd of tiny specks came surging in.

"And still they come, at Liane's command," she laughed. "They are those who played, to disarm your suspicions, at blocking your entry to this place. They did but follow you, a safe distance behind."

"I thought so," murmured Correy. "Things were going too smoothly. That was what we heard, sir."

I nodded, and looked up at Liane.

"You have many followers," I said. "Yet this is but a small world, and behind the Council are all the worlds of the universe."

Liane threw back her head and laughed, a soft, tinkling sound that rose clearly above the hollow roar of the mighty flame behind her throne.

"You speak bravely," she said, "knowing that Liane holds the upper hand. Did your Council take armed action against us, we would blow up these caverns which are the source of your precious temite, and bury it so deeply no force that could live here could extract it in the quantities in which the universe needs it.

"But enough of this exchange of sharp words. Liane has already said that she is disposed to be gracious. Does that not content you?"

"I will bear back to those who sent me whatever word you have to offer; it is not for me to judge its graciousness," I said coolly.

"Then—but first, let me show you how well I rule here," she said. She spoke to one of the old men seated at her feet; he arose and disappeared in a passage leading from directly beneath the dais.

"You will see, presently, the punishment of Liane," she said smilingly. "Liane, Chief Priestess of the Flame, Mother of Life, Giver of Death, Most Worshiped of the Worshipers.

"Perhaps you wonder how it came that Liane sits here in judgment upon a whole people? Let me tell you, while we await the execution of Liane's judgment.

"The father of Liane, and his father before him, back unto those remote days of which we have no knowledge, were Chief Priests of the Worshipers of the Flame. But they were lacking in ambition, in knowledge, and in power. Their followers were but few, and their hands were held out in benediction and not in command.

"But the father of Liane had no son; instead he had a daughter, in whom was all the wisdom of those who had been the Chief Priests. She gathered about her a group of old men, shrewd and cunning, the lesser priests and those who would know the feel of power, who were not priests. You see them here at the feet of Liane.

"And under Liane's guidance, the ranks of the Worshipers grew, and as this power grew, so grew the power of Liane, until the time came when no man, no woman, on the face of Lakos, dared question the command of the Chief Priestess. And those who would have rebelled, were made to feel the power of Liane—as these you see here now."

The old man had reappeared, and behind him were two miserable wretches, closely guarded by a dozen armed men. Liane spoke briefly to the old man, and then turned to us.

"The first of these is one who has dared to disobey," she explained. "He brought out more of the ore than Liane had ordered. Do you hear the multitude? They know already what his fate will be."

A long, shuddering whisper had arisen from the thousands of beings crouched there in the amphitheater, as the uncouth figure of the prisoner was led up a flight of steep, narrow steps to the very base of the flame.

Hendricks, still hiding his face from us, bent over Liane and whispered something in her ear; she caressed his arm softly, and shook her head. Hendricks leaned more heavily against the throne, shuddering.

Slowly, the flame was dying, until we could see that it was not a solid pillar of fire, but a hollow circle of flame, fed by innumerable jets set at the base of a circle of a trifle more than the length of a man across.

Into those deadly circles the condemned man was led. His legs were bound swiftly, so that he could not move, and the old man stepped back quickly.

As though his movement had been a signal, the flames shot up with a roar, until they lost themselves far over our heads. As one man, the three of us started forward, but the guards hemmed us in instantly.

"Fools!" cried Liane. "Be still! The power of Liane is absolute here."

We stared, fascinated, at the terrible sight. The flame spouted, streaks of blue and yellow streaking up from its base. Mercifully, we could not see within that encircling wall of fire.

Slowly, the flame died down again. A trap-door opened in the circle, and some formless thing dropped out of sight. Liane questioned the old man again, her eyes resting upon the other prisoner. The old man answered briefly.

"This one spoke against the power of Liane," she explained smilingly. "He said Liane was cruel; that she was selfish. He also must feel the embrace of the sacred Flame."

I heard, rather than saw, the ghastly drama repeated, for I had bent my head, and would not look up. Liane was no woman; she was a fiend. And yet for her a trusted officer, a friend, had forsworn his service and his comrades. I wondered, as I stood there with bowed head, what were the thoughts which must have been passing through Hendricks' mind.

"You fear to look upon the punishment of Liane?" the voice of the unholy priestess broke in upon my shuddering reverie. "Then you understand why her power is absolute; why she is Mother of Life, and Giver of Death, throughout all Lakos. And now for the word I promised you, a gracious word from one who could be terrible and not gracious, were that her whim.

"It has been in the mind of Liane to extend her power, to make for herself a place in this Supreme Council of which you speak with so much awe and reverence, Commander Hanson. But, by happenchance, another whim has seized her."

Liane looked up at Hendricks, smilingly, and took one of his hands in hers. It was wonderful how her face softened as he returned, fiercely, the pressure of her soft hands.

"I know it will sound strange to your ears," she said in a voice almost tender, "but Liane is, after all, a woman, with many, if not all, a woman's many weaknesses. And while even in his presence Liane will say that her lover was at the beginning looked upon as no more than a tool which might further Liane's power, he has won now a place in her heart."

I saw Hendricks tremble as she admitted her love, and that portion of his face which we could see flushed hotly.

"And so, Liane has elected to give up, at least for the present, the place in the Council which she could command. For after all, that would be a remote power, lacking in the elements of physical power which Liane has over these, her people, and in which she has learned to delight.

"So, Commander Hanson, bear to your superiors this word: Liane will permit a production of whatever reasonable amount of temite is desired. She will remain here with her consort, brooking no interference, no changes, no commands from any person or organization. Go, now, and take with you the words of Liane!"

I looked up at her gravely, and shook my head.

"We shall go," I said, "and we shall take with us your words. But I warn you that the words you have spoken are treason to the universe, in that you have defied the Council!"

Liane leaped from her throne, her scarlet lips drawn back against her white and gleaming teeth. Her eyes, dilated with anger, blazed down upon us almost as hotly as the flame which rose behind her.

"Go! And quickly!" she fairly screamed. "If you have no desire to feel the embrace of the sacred Flame, then *go*!"

I bowed silently, and motioned to Correy and Kincaide. Swiftly, we made our way down a long aisle, surrounded by motionless figures staring unwinkingly at the column of fire, toward the door by which we had entered this great chamber.

Behind us, I could hear Liane's clear voice lifted in her own guttural language, as she addressed the multitude.

Safely within the *Ertak*, we discussed the morning's adventure over a late luncheon.

"I suppose," said Kincaide, "there's nothing left to do but tell Fetter as much as seems wise, to reassure him, and then return to Base to make our report."

"We'll come back, if we do," growled Correy. "And we'll come back to *fight*. The Council won't stand for her attitude."

"Undoubtedly that's true," I admitted. "Still, I believe we should put it up to Base, and through Base to the Council, before doing anything more. Much, if not all, of what she said was perfectly true."

"It was that," nodded Kincaide. "There were scores, if not hundreds of doors leading into that big chamber; I imagine it can be reached, underground, from any point on the continent. And those winding passages would be simple to defend from any form of invasion."

"But could these Lakonians fight?" asked Correy. "That's what I'd like to know. I doubt it. They look like a sleepy, ignorant lot."

"I think they'd fight, to the death, if Liane ordered them to," I replied thoughtfully. "Did you notice the way they stared at the flame, never moving, never even winking? My idea is that it exercises a sort of auto-hypnotic influence over them, which gives Liane just the right opportunity to impress her will upon them."

"I wondered about that," Kincaide commented. "I believe you're right, sir. Any idea as to when we'll shove off?"

"There's no particular hurry; Fetter will be busy until evening, I imagine, so we won't bother him until then. As soon as we've had a chat with him, we can start."

"And without Hendricks," said Kincaide, shaking his head sadly. "I wonder—"

"If you don't mind, Mr. Kincaide, we won't mention his name on the *Ertak* after this," I interrupted. "I, for one, would rather forget him. Wouldn't you?"

"I would, sir, if I could," said Kincaide softly. "But that's not easy, is it?"

It wasn't easy. As a matter of fact, it was impossible. I knew I would never forget my picture of him, standing there shaken and miserable, beside the woman for whom he had disgraced his uniform, hiding his head in shame from the eyes of the men he had called comrades, and who had called him friend. But to talk of him was morbid.

It was late in the afternoon when I called Correy and Kincaide to the navigating room, where I had spent several hours charting our return course.

"I believe, gentlemen," I remarked, "that we can call on Mr. Fetter now. I'll ask you to remain in charge of the ship, Mr. Kincaide, while Mr. Correy and I—"

An attention signal sounded sharply to interrupt me. I answered it instantly.

"Sentry at exit, sir," said an excited voice. "Mr. Hendricks and the woman stowaway are here asking for you. They say it is very urgent."

"Bring them both here at once, under guard," I ordered. "Be sure you are properly relieved."

"Right, sir!"

I turned to Correy and Kincaide, who were watching me with curious eyes. My excitement must have shown upon my face.

"Mr. Hendricks and Liane are at the exit, asking to see me," I snapped. "They'll be here in a moment. What do you suppose is in the air?"

"Hendricks?" muttered Correy, his face darkening. "It seems to me he has a lot of nerve to—"

There was a sharp tap on the door.

"Come!" I ordered quickly. The door opened and Liane, followed by Hendricks, hurried into the room.

"That will do," I nodded to the guard who had accompanied them. "You may go."

"You wonder why we're here, I suppose?" demanded Liane. "I'll tell you, quickly, for every instant is precious."

This was a very different Liane. She was no longer clad in diaphanous black; she was wearing a tunic similar to the one she had worn on board the *Ertak*, save that this one was torn and soiled. Her lips, as she talked, twitched with an insane anger; her amazing eyes were like those of a cornered beast of the wilderness.

"My council of wise old men turned against me when I told them my plans to marry the man of my choice. They said he was an outsider, an enemy, a foreigner. They would have none of him. They demanded that I give him to the Flame, and marry one of my own kind. They had not, of course, understood what I had said to you there in the great chapel of the Flame.

"I defied them. We escaped through a passage which is not known to any save myself, and the existence of which my father taught me years ago. We are here, but they will guess where we have gone. My old men are exciting my people against me—and for that shall all, down to the last one, know the embrace of the Flame!" She gritted her teeth on the words, her nostrils distended with rage.

"I—I am safe. I can command them; I can make them know my power, and I shall. The Flame will have much to feed upon in the days which are to come, I promise you. But my beloved would not be safe; at this moment I cannot protect him. So I have brought him back. I—I know he ... but I will not be weak. I am Liane!"

She faced Hendricks, who had stood there like a graven image, watching her. Her arms went about his neck; her lips sought his.

"My beloved!" she whispered. "Liane was but a woman, after all. Darling! Good-by!" She kissed him again, and hurried to the door.

"One more thing!" she cried. "I must master them myself. I must show them I—I, Liane—am ruler here. You promise? You promise me you will not interfere; that you will do nothing?"

"But—"

Liane interrupted me before I could put my objections into words.

"Promise!" she commanded. "There are hundreds, thousands of them! You cannot slay them all—and if you did, there would be more. I can bend them to my will; they know my power. Promise, or there will be many deaths upon your hands!"

"I promise," I said.

"And you—all of you?" she demanded, sweeping Correy and Kincaide with her eyes.

"Commander Hanson speaks for us all," nodded Kincaide.

With a last glance at Hendricks, whose eyes had never left her for an instant, she was gone.

Hendricks uttered a long, quivering sigh. His face, as he turned to us, was ghastly white.

"She's gone," he muttered. "Forever."

"That's exceedingly unfortunate, sir, for you," I replied crisply. "As soon as it's perfectly safe, we'll see to it that you depart also."

The sting of my words apparently did not touch him.

"You don't understand," he said dully. "I know what you think, and I do not blame you. She came back; you know that.

"'You are coming with me,' she said. 'I care for you. I want you. You are coming with me, at once.' I told her I was not; that I loved her, but that I could not, would not, go.

"She opened a port and showed me one of her countrymen, standing not far away, watching the ship. He held something in his hand.

"'He has one of your hand bombs,' she told me. 'I found it while I was hidden and took it with me when I left. If you do not come with me, he will throw it against the ship, destroy it, and those within it.'

"There was nothing else for me to do. She permitted me to explain no more than I did in the note I left. I pleaded with her; did all I could. Finally I persuaded her to give you the word she did, there before the great flame.

"She brought me back here at the risk of her own life, and, what is even more precious to her, her power. In—in her own way, she loves me...."

It was an amazing story; a second or two passed before any of us could speak. And then words came, fast and joyous; our friend, our trusted fellow-officer had come back to us! I felt as though a great black cloud had slid from across the sun.

And then, above our voices, rose a great mutter of sound. We glanced at one another, wonderingly. Hendricks was the first to make a move.

"That's the mob!" he said, darting toward the door. We followed him swiftly to the exit of the ship, through the air-lock, out into the open.

Hendricks had spoken the truth. Liane was walking, very slowly and deliberately, her head flung back proudly, toward the city. Coming toward her, like a great ragged wave, was a mighty mass of humanity, led by capering old men—undoubtedly the lesser priests, who had turned against her.

"The portable projectors, sir!" begged Correy excitedly. "A pair of them, and that mob—"

"We're bound by our promise," I reminded him. "She's not afraid; her power is terrible. I believe she'll win without them. Look!"

Liane had paused. She lifted one hand in a gesture of command, and called out to the rabble. Correy translated the whole thing for me later.

"Halt!" she cried sharply. "Who moves upon the Chief Priestess of the Flame earns the embrace of the Flame!"

The crowd halted, cowering; then the old man shouted to them and gestured them onward. With a rush, the front ranks came on.

"So!" Liane called out to them. "You would disobey Liane? Yet even yet it is not too late; Liane gives you one chance more. You little know the Chief Priestess of the Flame if you think she will tolerate an encroachment of her power. Back! Back, I say, or you all shall feel the might of Liane!"

Before her tirade the mob faltered, but again the crazed old men led them on.

Liane turned, saw us, and made a regal gesture of farewell. From the bosom of her tunic she snatched a small black object, and swung it high above her head.

"The bomb!" shouted Hendricks. "She has it; she—"

At the very feet of the onrushing crowd the black object struck. There was a hollow roar; a blast of thundering air swept us backward to the ground.

When we scrambled to our feet, Liane was gone. The relentless mob had gone. Where they had been was a great crater of raw earth, strewn with ghastly fragments. Far back toward the city a few straggling figures ran frantically away from that scene of death.

"Gone!" I said. "Power was a mania, an obsession with her. Even her death was a supreme gesture—of power, of authority."

"Liane," Hendricks whispered. "Chief Priestess of the Flame ... Giver of Death...."

With Liane gone, and with her the old men who had tried to snatch her power from her hand, and who might have caused us trouble, the rebellion of the Lakonians was at an end.

Leaderless, they were helpless, and I believe they were happy in the change. Sometimes the old ways are better than the new, and Liane's régime had been merciless and rather terrible.

There are many kinds of women: great women, and women with small souls; women filled with the spirit of sacrifice; selfish women, good women and bad.

And Liane? I leave her for you to judge. She was a woman; classify her for yourself.

After all, I am an old man, and perhaps I have forgotten the ways of women. I do not wish to judge, on one hand to be called bitter and hard, on the other hand to be condemned as soft with advancing age.

I have given you the story of Liane, Chief Priestess of the Flame.

How, you clever and infallible members of this present generation, do you judge her?

Milton Keynes UK
Ingram Content Group UK Ltd.
UKHW050648260624
444769UK00004B/169